A KID IN THE FUNERAL

PRIYASH SORENG

For all those who lost their loved ones and also the survivors of this COVID-19 pandemic.

We all are together in this.

Contents

Preface

Hello, to whomsoever reading this, myself Priyash Soreng. I thought to address this matter since we all have somewhat or somehow suffered through this pandemic, despite the intensity which ranges for each individual. During this time, I have seen multiple deaths of my loved ones, which made me realize the fact of self-worth. A new revelation was sparked in me when one day I saw a hearse, which took my inner-being back in time, when I saw it the last time. It made me realize that really 'life is too short'. I think in this 'fast-paced world' we all are lacking the essence of 'moral values' in our lives, which is, not to mention, equally important and should be passed on. This is why I thought that I want to encourage and motivate you all, especially the 'Gen Z' and also the upcoming ones. And, I also think now is the perfect time, because it's either Now or Never. I have chosen this topic especially to highlight the two different perception of life. I made sure that my story is short and simple – not too lengthy so that you would get lost in between and also to avoid any distortion in the flow of the theme. The excerpt in [] describes the audio profile in order to create background setting, so that you can properly visualize the elements. Also, I want to address that I made sure the narration and also the characters themselves are gender inclusive, which is also a serious issue in today's world. I wanted to make sure all of us can relate to this story, with each character, without feeling it to be gender biased. In the entire story you'll find gender neutral pronouns such as (*they/them/theirs*) in italic fonts to address a singular and non-binary person. I hope you have good read and also a good day.

Acknowledgements

I wish to acknowledge, because I am extremely grateful, to all my friends and family, who were always there of me, throughout this 'emotional ride', in my highs and lows. They sat down with me and to discuss the matter; listened and also maintained the sanity.

Ultimately thanks to all who are reading this book, I appreciate your support too.

Thank you, sending love and happiness to all.

CHAPTER ONE

Heavy breathing. [Panting]. Heartbeat pumps and suddenly stops. [ECG Beeps and stops]. [Flat lining]. Blur vision turns black. Body starts to feel light. The voices around me tend to fade and I can barely speak. For a moment I am at a loss to realize what is it? It all feels like a dream – a nightmare we fear to come true. What is it, after all? Have you ever felt it? It feels like a deep sleep or hibernation of some kind.

My fingers go numb. I cannot feel them – as if they are no longer part of me. Moreover, there is this feeling of something huge lying over my back, like it's pressing me down such that I won't be able to stand. A mixed feeling of everything I've been through has swirled like a cyclone in sea of subconscious. It's something I cannot understand at the moment. My mind is blank. Flashes of blur visions with a light glare want to capture the image, but it is as if the human body's all-powerful mind is resisting it.

Well! I open my eyes and find myself in a dark place. As I move forward, I seem to have been hit by a wall after 3 steps. Therefore by touching the walls with my bare hands I move to right. But the same happened, so I move to the right again, and again until I realize that I am coffined in a box. I am caught up by a panic attack as I am claustrophobic. I am just not able to breathe. The anxiety has taken over me and I slowly pass out. [Body thuds].

Gradually, I feel a disconnection from my body as if my whole body is being swallowed up – completely being devoured. Later, I find myself hovering around in dead space. Feels like hallucination. Floating here and there, as if I am in a stream, I have to rely totally on the flow, since I can only see but not move. Not much later, the flow turns wild like it is ravenous and wants to eat me up, but unfortunately I cannot move. Soon the waves roll over and over and I am just drowning in them. I think that I am gone, but then nonchalantly, I come to my senses and as I look around, I can see a wormhole. I have never seen a wormhole except in the movie – Interstellar, but I can see it now. Slowly..., I go deeper into sleep as I move into the wormhole. I can see stars and clouds all around, but all of a sudden [Bang] the ground sinks and everything falls in it. Falling down I screamed, but it is inaudible; all I can feel is my body becoming lighter. [Inaudible scream]

Suddenly, I wake up and realize that I was gone for about five minutes. It is pitch-black everywhere – not even the faintest glimmer of light shines here. But somewhere, far beyond I can hear some voices, faint voices. So, I start running towards them. While running, I feel no tiredness; it is like I have been trained for wining gold in Olympics. A sprint making a slit in the air as well as closing it behind, I keep running and slowly I can see the finish line. While running, as I look around, I can see visions of my past events – my childhood, my adulthood – yet I keep running. Even if I want to stop, my legs didn't stop running. The closer I reach the voices; the more I can hear them – they sound like people are crying. The amplitude increases, the closer I go. Upon reaching the finish line, the voices fade away and I come across a black window. Here, I can see my friends and my *parents* waiting for me, but sadly they are about to leave. I reach out to them and [Cracks] the window cracks [Continue cracking]. All of a sudden, the voices surround me, making it difficult for me to locate where the origin of the voices is. As far as one can see, all they can see is darkness – coal black. And suddenly…, I can hear someone, a voice so familiar to me that I couldn't possibly forget. I turn back but the voices now became loud – so deafening that I can barely hear, hence I cover my ears. [Both – the magnitude and frequency increase and fades].

It's weird. Everything that just happened I am not sure whether it was a dream or a reality [Opening eyes]. And all of sudden, in front of my eyes I could see myself, or an image of me, right there sleeping. Sleeping with no concern about anything as someone would kiss as an antidote to a sleeping poison. The crying voices continue again, however this time they are loud and clear. I look around and it is something that I never wanted to see at the first place. [Suspenseful music]

CHAPTER TWO

[*Child* giggling] You see there, that's me, a child born with good health in an unconditionally loving family. And my *parents* [*Parent 1*: - "Oh there you are my *child*, how much I missed you today"; *Parent 2*: - "Our *child* is growing fond of you and usually cries when you leave"]... such lovely and kind beings. They were always there for me, whether I noticed it or not. From the day I started walking, to the day I rode my first bicycle, from the day I won the essay competition, to the day I failed in Mathematics, my *parents* were always by my side. Growing up in a middle-class family, I have always dreamt of doing something bigger in my life, to make my *parents* proud. In school, I wasn't the ace student, just an average. I also made some good friends around there. Usually, we used to go to school together, eat lunch together, and play together. Throwing birthday parties, going to the beach at summer, playing video games, getting our shoes soggy in the rain, going to the fair, doing a movie marathon, making each other a holiday present and eating the Christmas cake together, all we did, was have fun and an amazing time. Nevertheless, it all went so quick that we didn't realize that soon we would be graduating from even High School. Post that our paths might get separated, but we decided to make all our paths merge one day. Some people say, 'God loves us so much that they provide us with guardian angels like our friends and family to protect us from harm'. And until now I thought this was life. [Cheerful music]

Time flies by so fast. Now some year later, we all got into different jobs. I ended up working in a multi-national company. I worked hard to fulfill all my dreams and desires, and all this boils down to that one moment – I climbed the ladder of success, and by dint of my hard-work, very soon become the President of my company. My friends and family were so happy and proud of my achievement. It was as though my vision board came alive. Some might say I hit a jackpot or perhaps it was just luck. Beside what they say, I felt lucky. But was I really lucky? It was not until sometime later that I actually became luckily-unlucky. I gradually stopped being an active participant in my friends' and family gatherings, owing to my harrowing work schedule. It's like what is so truly stated 'With great power comes great responsibilities' or 'Uneasy lies the head that wears the crown'. One has to sacrifice something in order to achieve something. Yet, I was okay with it. Except for one day, my company sales dropped down and we suffered heavy losses in the market. It was a time of crisis for me and my company. Working over-time was the need of the hour; in addition to that my work-life balance went for a toss. I slowly started losing my friends because I barely communicated with people. But I was okay with it, because I could later make it up to them.

Everything in my life was tied by a string; if anything falls, it will take everything down with it. Something very tragic occurred in my life. I lost my *parents* in a car accident and I couldn't do anything to save them. Who would have actually thought that they would lose people this way? Who can understand the misery of losing near and dear one like this? I could see my beautiful world shattering right before my eyes. Life hit me hard like a wrecking ball. All I could see was my entire empire, which I had built with my sweat and blood, rumbling down, getting torn and break into thousands of pieces, while I was just standing there and looking at those broken pieces, with a bleeding heart, feeling numb and helpless as the waves of chaos hit me like a tsunami. Now this was the life I wasn't prepared for.

A few years late, we finally could reestablish and restore our company back to normalcy. With that, we bounced back and brought back our past glory, that of being the top amongst many companies in the entire continent. Well, good news. Ain't it? Yes, few materialistic things can be restored, but what about my losses? Was that good? Can we consider it to be, good? Doesn't it matter? It does. But can I go back and change things, make it any better? Could I have done something? Can I do anything? Why did it happen and happen only to me? Why just me? Why? I haven't talked about it with anyone in years. Never in my life had I felt so vulnerable. All I feel now is a sense of shame and guilt as I regret for every move and every decision I have taken. I feel lost. I don't feel myself anymore. It is like I have lost my entity. I now live all alone and depressed, being wasted. Now my life is vain and void.

After all, what I went through, moving on seemed difficult, especially with all those traumatizing events haunting me. Clinging back to the past always makes one feel guilty and also weak and empty. Now, all that matters is me, as I have my dreams to fulfill. I have a life ahead of me. With this confidence I live my life until today.

Today, as I gallantly stride down the hallway, to get into this special meeting which I am so sure will give an extra boost to my company's sales, all of a sudden I hear a beep, loud and clear, and then it stops. I am just not able to feel my body and I fall down with a thud. [ECG beeps and stops]

CHAPTER THREE

... I look around and it is something that I never wanted to see at the first place. It's the sight which broke me, despite the fact that I was already broken. How does the mirror itself feel when it's broken? Does it hurt? After undergoing everything, after all what could possibly hurt me now? I was so moved by what I saw, as if my soul drifted out of my body. It felt like the last ounce of blood just dropped out from my heart as it was grated, yet I didn't feel any pain. Well! What was it? It was something we all fear – the very thought sends chill down the spine – one's own death. As if that was not enough, all those voices I was overhearing were voices of people who cared for me in that world – the world which I am no longer a part of. I have been taken away from the people I belong. Eventually, and sadly, I lost everything, and now, even all of me. My life used to be vain and void; now I'm vain and void. Could I have done something? Can I do anything? I literally don't know. What could I possibly do? It felt as if the floor beneath me just slipped and I sank in it with everything that was mine. For that one moment, I still couldn't believe if it was a nightmare or reality. Besides I could hear people whisper so I went to talk to them but before I could, I heard Church bells ringing because it's time for the Funeral. [Church bells ringing]

It's like what the famous American film director Woody Allen had said, "It's not that I'm afraid to die, I just don't want to be there when it happens." Yet no one knows when death beckons us and none is ready when it embraces. This was so sudden – something I had never predicted. Thought I would be enjoying my last days of my life in a countryside farmhouse, watching football, listening to vinyl records, watching sunset, cooking my favorite meal before going to my deathbed and praying that my death would be painless. Except for now, I am here standing amidst of all people. What a pathetic sight – watching yourself dead there and the ones who care and loves you are crying over, yet you can't even wipe their tears. How could I not be moved? Even if I want to cry now, where are my tears? My emotions are all numb. How can you be 'sad', and can't shed tears? How can I show that it hurts me? It is not worth it. I feel pity for myself. Moreover, I hear people talking about what a good person I was. Was I? A good person? I don't think so. Because I remember how 'actually' good I was. I never talked with anyone and always ill-behaved with them even though it was my fault. I never apologized, never made it up to them. But what all they did was because they were concerned, up until now. But was I worthy? My friends – the only ones I have in my life are still here with me, but what did I do for them, I never enjoyed my life with them, and at this very moment, look where am I? When my *parents* died, I was also dead to the world. I just ghosted people like my whole existence just vanished. But still they all were there for me, holding me up so that I won't go rogue and do something wrong that might hurt me. Such a lot of generosity – Why? I had been a terrible person and yet they say I was good. Do I deserve it? All my eyes could see are the visions of past events. Some horrific, some emotional, some terrifying but none of them were good. [Objects clattering][Shouting in anger][Threatening][Door opens and slams].

People come to realize their own worth only after they die; the expanse of love that people in their life have for them, that's the 'worth'. But why do we wait so long to realize this? There are so many people in this funeral – more than I anticipated. As I look around, I see people who have come to pay their homage and to bid a final goodbye. Some of them are close ones, some are far ones, some I rarely visited and some of them I don't even recognize. But amongst them there was something or someone unusual, a *kid* in *their* early teens, petite, of medium height, thin frame and a face with a familiar look, also crying as if something precious of *theirs* is lost. The sight of the *kid* filled the dead me with pity. Sobbing hard *their* face had become pale. The *kid* is trying to say something but *their* voice cracks, so I get closer. Looking towards the pit, in shaky voice the *kid* says, "D.....do...yo..you.....remember....me?"[Suspenseful music] Do I know this *kid*? *Their* face looks familiar, but who is this *kid*? Have we ever met? Thoughts cloud my mind.

CHAPTER FOUR

"Remember: -the ability to do something or bring one's mind into awareness of something or someone from the past."

After I lost my *parents* and also when things weren't good at work too, I was totally broken. I have always looked for ways to channelize my emotions, to put the dead weight down, to get it off my chest so that I could finally breathe. I have become restless since I had to work overtime. This made it difficult for me to find time to relax. So, I started visiting a bar, which was on my way home and continues to open till late night, for a drink. It was a small bar and people frequented this place. I could faintly remember having me this *kid* there for about 2-3 times. But who is this *kid*?

One day after a crazy-day at work, I came to this place and I was sitting at the counter, waiting for my order to be taken, when I saw this juvenile teenage *kid* with black wavy hair and gleaming eyes coming towards me. With youthful voice *they* say, "What do you want to order, *Mx*?" And I reply, "Barbera: – The Classic Italian Red Wine". With a winsome smile on *their* face, *they* took my order. Though not with any mal-intent of prying on *their* personal life and I don't want to deject *them* but I couldn't resist but asked *them*, "Why this work? What do your *parents* do? Do they know about this?" And as I started this volley of questions, I could see *their* smile turning upside down. It was like I had broken the remaining fixed-pieces of *theirs*. With watery eyes, *they* said, "I have nowhere to go, nowhere to be. I have been fired from 6 other places. In fact this job is my least priority but it pays me well." I still didn't understand the reason why at the age of studying *they* choose to work in the first place. I didn't want to interrupt but then *they* continued " I belong to a family that comes from a very low economic background, my *parents* got divorced and I live with one of *parent* and two little *siblings*" "In order to earn a decent income to ensure my little *siblings* could go to school, I took up jobs like this" I wanted to apologize to *them*, but *they* carried on "How's your work going, I so much admire you, I'm fascinated by your work. I had read it an article in a local newspaper" "How does it feel to be successful? Fulfilling your dream? Is it good?" And I replied, "It's good to be successful, to achieve what you dreamt about". *They* then continued "Of-course! You must be happy. You get what you want". At that moment, I possibly couldn't say anything, but to pretend that I was happy. Who knows what goes in a person's mind. I just smiled, patted *them* and then left.

One night, when I met the *kid* again in the bar, *they* looked very distressed so I asked *them* "You good? Did something happen?" and *they* said, "The *parent* I'm living with has been diagnosed with leukemia and we don't have enough money for *their* medication and treatment". I was stunned when *they* said that, so I asked *them* if I could do anything to help, but *they* refused my help. I couldn't hire *them* too, since *they* were pretty young. All the same, I wanted to do something for *them*, so I gave *them* a huge tip and left

The next time when I was there, I wanted to meet the *kid* and ask *them* about *their parent*. But when I asked *them*, *they* said that *their parent* is doing well however *they* didn't take the money and gave it to *their manager*. And when I asked why, *they* said, "I work here with dignity; I get paid for what I do, not because of my circumstances". I was amazed by this response and told *them*, "It's true that money can't save people". "I have also lost people, the good and near ones too, and since then my life has become meaningless without them". The *kid* asked "Who did you lose?" so I told *them* about my friends and family. And *they* said, "What did you do?". At first I didn't understand, so *they* continued "What did you do, to make things right? You didn't lose your friends, forever, did you?" And I said, "They didn't understand my workload, also I needed to make good amount of money before I could travel the world with them" "After my *parents*, they were there, but I distanced myself." "I know I was wrong but I could not do anything about it". Hearing this, the *kid* replied, "If it hurts you, why don't you apologize and make up to them, after all it does matter to you." "If you have to take risk, now is the time, you live once and you die once" "Also, if you always wish to have more, you will never be satisfied with 'enough'" Those words hit me hard and I said "I know what I'm doing, I don't need any advice from a *child*" "And if it hurts my friends too, then why don't they approach me". The *kid* quietly listened but continued again, "I wanted to help you because all my life I have looked for a *parental-figure*" "You know why my *parents* got divorced, because one my *parent*, who doesn't reside with us, was arrogant and greedy. *They* only thought of themselves. Now *they* have lost us-the only people in this world *they* had, nonetheless it doesn't matter to *them*". "But you still got time; God is merciful to you about this." And while the *kid* was speaking, I watched *their* face as tear rolled down through *their* cheeks.

Oh! And yes, yes I remember this *kid*, except its too late now. The time for me has arrived and I cannot go back.

CHAPTER FIVE

" "They say such nice things about people in funerals that it makes me sad that I'm going to miss mine by just few days." (Garrison Keillor: – American Author)"

The ceremony has begun and they are ready to perform for the funeral rites: - The Burial. [Clergy: - "We have all gathered here to join for the final mourning of our beloved...]. Death: - the final stage of all living beings, a state which is unaltered and irreversible. Is death that good? While living on that beautiful earth, I didn't do much 'good'. I was a narcissist and now I'm nothingness. My entire life I have hurt *people*, made them feel nothing but weak, made them realize how bad they were. But was I good? I am a bad, or worse, a terrible *person*. I have only broken and damaged the remaining pieces of people's lives that they had collected. At this very moment, especially after death, I don't want to feel for not living up to my life or to other's expectations. I wish I could have been a better *person*. I wish I wouldn't have to abandon people. I wish that I could have been more open and vulnerable to my friends. I wish that I would have packed my bag that day and would have gone with my friends. I wish that I wouldn't have been this greedy. I wish that I should have been satisfied with 'enough'. I wish that I shouldn't have yelled at people for helping me. I wish that I should have asked for forgiveness soon. I wish that I should have spent time with my folks. I wish that I should have listened to the *kid*. I wish that I could have been a better *person* for *them*. I wish that I wouldn't have hurt *them*. But only if, if, I could go back in time and make things right, once and for all, which I think I should have done before. Yet look at those noble people; wish I would have been there to comfort them. After everything I did to them, they are still here. Why? Because they love me, the unconditional love they have for me. I was never alone in this sphere with billions of people. But if I would have been a better *person* and been good to others, I would have actually died in peace, leaving behind any ties or strings that would connect me back to that world, like what the actual R. I. P. would mean. But I can't do anything about it, as like every other soul I must move on.

'We all know, we can't stop things like this from happening. We were born to live this life and we live this life to die. It's all natural. But you know what, the beauty about death is that there is no more pain, no more grief and no more death. It's a cycle. We become a part of who we are, joining our ancestors and waiting for the upcoming generation. We are art – a masterpiece – that serves the Maker. We never know when death is going to knock our doors, until then we still have a life, to nourish ourselves'. If given a chance, this would have been my eulogy. [Heaven pours rain][The casket is lowered into the ground][People scattering soil over the casket] [People sobbing][People paying tributes][Funeral hymns play in background].

""From my rotting body, flowers shall grow and I am in them, and that is eternity." (Edvard Munch: – Norwegian Painter)"

Every one's life ends in the same way, but the way *they* have lived their life and how *they* die is what makes one's story different from others. I wish that if, just if, I lived my life taking risk, fearless of making mistakes and also learning and embracing them, living my life to its fullest potential, just for once, instead of being a scared, safe-playing and closeted person, I would have found my purpose, the meaning of my life and would be recalling those moments instead of feeling overwhelmed with regret.

Make your life count, make yourself worth to be living, make your voice stand out, and make yourself matter. Be unique, be the reason for the change you want to see, be that change, be kind, be acceptable, be helpful, be lovable, be generous, be optimistic because there is always a bigger picture, be who you are and be humane.

""Many people die at twenty-five and aren't buried until they are seventy-five." (Benjamin Franklin: – American polymath)"

Be like such people. Be an exemplar – be a good memory to others. Forgive and forget, life is too short to carry your enemies in your mind everywhere you go, this is how civilized as well as well-learned people live.

""Remember that people are only guests in your story- the same way you are only a guest in theirs- so make chapters worth reading." (Lauren Klarfled)"

Have fun because most of us may not even have that golden opportunity. Take a good amount of great memory to the ground. [Clergy: - As the Father said to Adam in the Garden of Eden, "...for you were made from dust, and to dust you shall return."(Genesis 3:19)]

"*PS: - "Live your life that the fear of death can never enter your heart." (Tecumseh: – a Shawnee chief and warrior)*"

- Priyash Soreng